Susan Hill

One Night a

Illustrated by
Vanessa Julian-Ottie

COLLINS
PICTURE LIONS

To Jessica, Tom and Harriet

First published in Great Britain 1984
by Hamish Hamilton Children's Books

First published in Picture Lions 1986

Picture Lions is an imprint of the Children's Division, part
of the Collin's Publishing Group, 8 Grafton Street,
London W1X 3LA.

Printed in Great Britain
by Warners (Midlands) plc, Bourne + London

Every Tuesday Tom and his mother went to the library. Inside, Tom's mother went one way to choose her books. And Tom went the other way to choose his.

He sat on a red chair at a red table and looked at a lot of books. When it was time to go, he could take six of them with him to read at home.

Sometimes he chose stories about old steam engines or racing cars…

sometimes about elephants or mice…

sometimes about boys like him…

Once he chose a book with stories about witches and goblins, and a great scaly dragon breathing fire out of its nostrils.

The next day Tom had a cold. He lay under a rug on the sofa and looked at his library books. He looked for a long time at the one about witches and goblins, and the great scaly dragon breathing fire out of its nostrils.

After that he thought he
would rather not be by himself,
so he went to the window
and called to his mother.

he came in. She said, "They're only
ictures in a book. They're not real.
'hey can't hurt you." "I know that,'
aid Tom "but it doesn't seem to
ake any difference."

That night Tom had a very bad dream. It was full of
witches and goblins, and the great scaly dragon
breathing fire out of its nostrils.

Tom woke up feeling hot and frightened. His
mother said, "It's because of your cold." She gave
him a drink of water and stayed with him for
a while.

On the table beside Tom's bed was a night-light. It had a spotty red shade like a toadstool. When Tom lay down and looked at the ceiling, he saw that the night-light made shadows there. The shadows had shapes. One shape was a witch's pointed nose, and another was a goblin's big ear.

The biggest, blackest shape was the head of the great scaly dragon. The shining light was like the fire it breathed out of its nostrils. Tom called to his mother. When she came she said, "We'd better take that book back to the library."

Every Thursday, Tom and his mother went to tea
with Tom's friend Ned.
Sometimes, Tom and Ned went
into the cupboard under the
stairs and made a pirates' den.

Sometimes they went up
the loft ladder and
looked at Ned's brother's
model aeroplanes.

Sometimes, on sunny days,
they sat with their feet
in the paddling pool
doing high kicks.

And sometimes, on wet days, they watched television. One day, when Tom had a cold, they watched a cartoon programme. It had a fox with a black mask and a red tongue, who was a robber.

That night, Tom had another very bad dream. He woke up feeling hot and frightened.

"It was about a fox with a black mask and a red tongue, who was a robber," he said.

"It wasn't real," said his mother. "It couldn't hurt you."

"I know that," said Tom, "but it doesn't seem to make any difference."

"Well, you'd better not watch any more cartoons on television," his mother said.

The next day, Tom's mother did the washing. Tom helped to put the dirty clothes into the machine.

Then he measured out the washing powder and put that in too.

Then he sat at the kitchen table and ate a piece of toast. The washing machine made a rumbling, bumbling, churning noise.

"It looks as if it's eating up the clothes, and now they're going round and round in its tummy," Tom thought.

When the clothes were washed, Tom helped his mother to hang them on the line in the back garden.

"There's a good breeze to dry them quickly," said his mother.

The breeze blew into Tom's father's white shirt and puffed it out and made the sleeves flap.

"That looks a bit ghosty," Tom said.

"Let's walk down to the shops now," said his mother.

On the way they passed
Mr Carter's house.
Mr Carter was outside
clipping the hedge.
"Hello, Mr Carter," said Tom.
"Hello there, young fellow-my-lad,"
said Mr Carter,
"How about a haircut?"

That night, Tom had another very bad dream. He woke up and called to his mother.

"There was a washing machine monster, and a ghosty shirt with clippers," Tom told her.

"We'd better have a look at those things in the morning," his mother said. So they did.

They looked at the
washing machine,
inside and outside.

They looked at Tom's
father's clean white shirt.

And they got out the hedge
clippers from the shed and
looked at those too.
"They're just ordinary
things," said Tom's mother.
"I know," said Tom, "but it
doesn't seem to make
any difference."

At bedtime, Tom's mother said,
"Shall we try and get rid of
those bad dreams?"
"Yes *please*," said Tom.
So his mother opened
the bedroom window.
"Out you go," she said.
"Away with you."
"Shoo!" said Tom in a fierce voice.
"Shoo, you bad old dreams."
And he flapped his arms
to chase them out of the window.

Then his mother closed it again.

"Now," she said, "I'm going to give you some good dreams. I've made them specially."

"Just like cakes," Tom said. And he got into bed.

"Close your eyes," said his mother.

Then she touched his eyelids very gently. She said, "Tonight you will have only those good dreams, and no bad ones at all."

"And shall I never have a bad dream again?" Tom asked.

"One night at a time," said his mother.

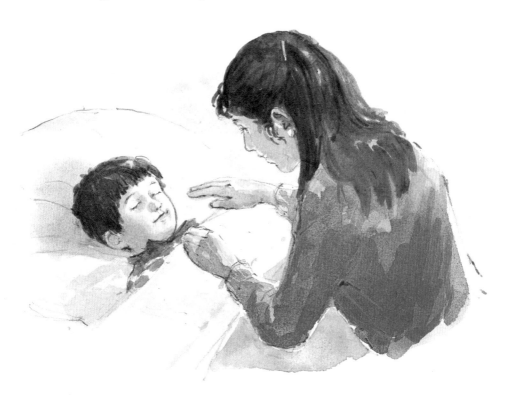

And that night, Tom did have only the good dreams, and no bad ones.

And the next night…   and the next…

But the night after
that, Tom's mother
had to go away to see his
grandfather.
"Daddy will look after you," she
told Tom.
"But what about my good dreams?" Tom asked her.
"*He* will give them to you, of course."
And he did.

Soon it was Tom's birthday. For his special treat,
Tom was going to stay overnight at Ned's house.
"I think you are old enough now," said his mother.

Tom packed his suitcase. He put in all the things he
would need, and quite a lot of things that he
wouldn't! He was very excited.

Ned had bunk beds in his room. He was going to sleep at the top and Tom was going to sleep at the bottom.

On Ned's bunk there was a large, brown, furry dog and a small, black, woolly dog.

"They are the watchdogs," Ned said.

When Tom's mother had gone, he and Ned helped make gingerbread men for tea.

Then they went into the garden to watch Ned's father make a bonfire.

At bedtime, Tom said, "Ned, what happens if you have bad dreams?"

"My watchdogs see them off," said Ned very sleepily.

But Tom wished he had reminded his mother to leave him some good dreams, before she went home.

He thought he might call out to Ned's mother. But he fell asleep instead.

That night, Tom did not have any dreams at all. He told his mother when he got home,
"I won't need you
to shoo the bad dreams out,
or give me any good ones,
ever again."
"I see," said his mother.
Tom felt very grown-up
and pleased.

That night he asked his mother to read him a story
about a giant. He hadn't wanted to look at that
book for quite a long time.

Afterwards, she tucked him in tightly and gave him
a kiss. Then Tom said, "Perhaps I had better have a
few good dreams. Just in case."

"I think that's a very good idea," said his mother.
And she gave them to him.

"But I won't need them tomorrow or ever after."

"One night at a time," said his mother.